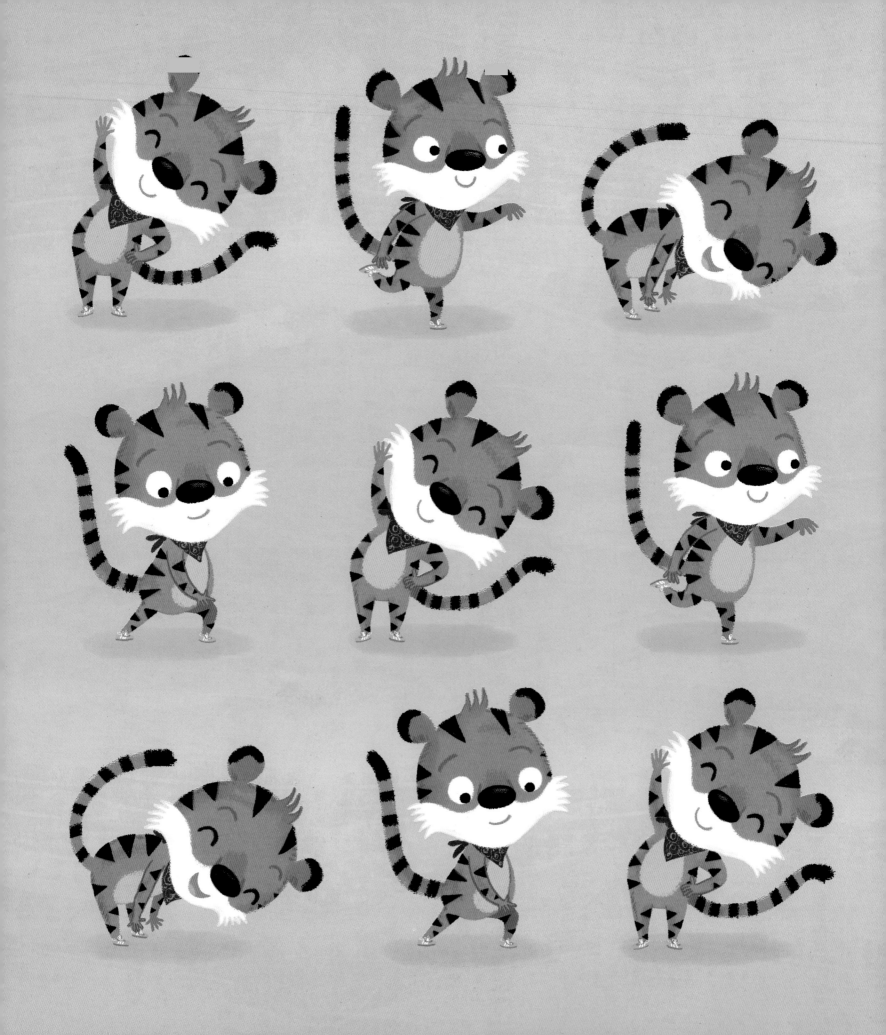

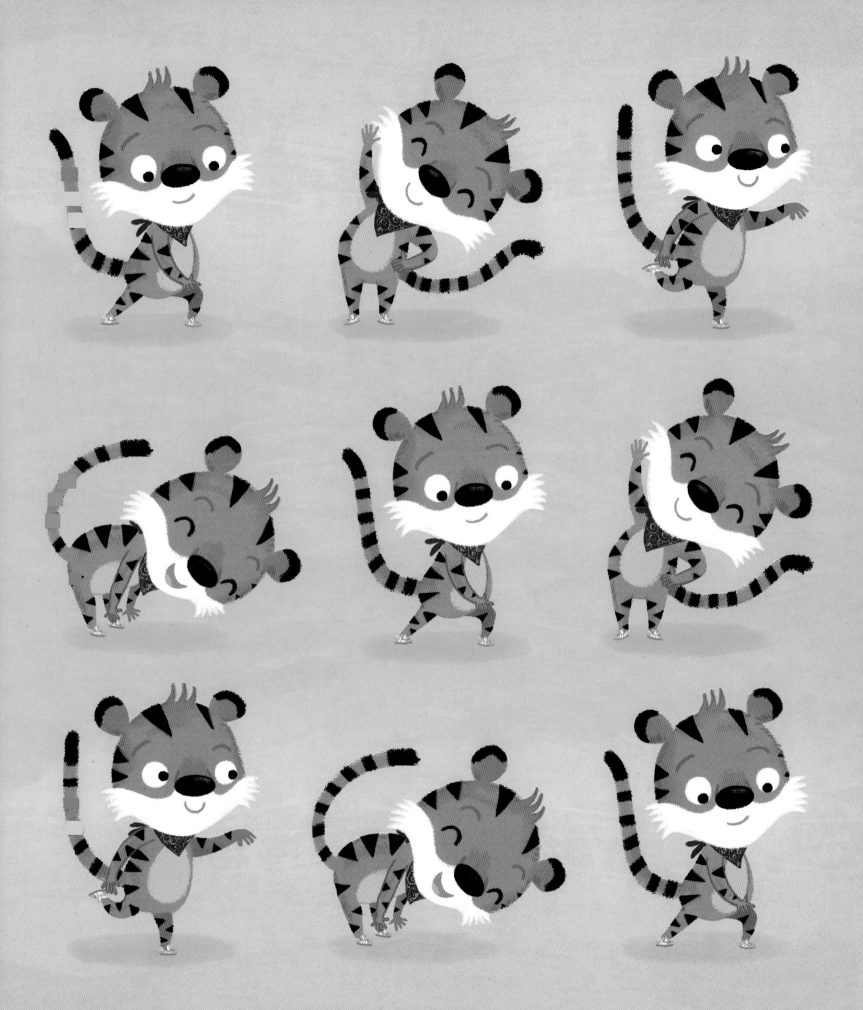

For Evie,
my favourite little person
V. G.

First published in 2016 by Scholastic Children's Books
Euston House, 24 Eversholt Street
London NW1 1DB
a division of Scholastic Ltd
www.scholastic.co.uk
London - New York - Toronto - Sydney - Auckland
Mexico City - New Delhi - Hong Kong

PB ISBN 978 1407 16428 1

Medal batch code: P09900

1 3 5 7 9 10 8 6 4 2

Gold Medal ME!

Vicki Gausden

SCHOLASTIC

It was a lovely, sunny day and Toby bounced out of bed.

Today was going to be a very special day at school – Sports Day.
There were going to be lots of races and games to play. Toby couldn't wait!

"Slow down with your breakfast!" smiled Toby's mum.
But Toby was in a bit of a rush...

"*Oops!*"

After breakfast, Toby found everything he needed for the day.

One red scarf…
his favourite!

Two super-speedy shoes…
perfect for running.

Three felt-tip pens…just in case!

Toby and his mum set off for school.

"Are we nearly there yet?" asked Toby excitedly.

Outside school, Toby met his friends Olivia Panda
and Charlie Cheetah. They talked about all
of the games they were going to play.

Sports Day

"I heard that Miss Meadow is going to give out
lots of **gold medals**," whispered Olivia.
"Wow!" Toby gasped. "I hope **I** get one."

When they got to the sports field, Toby could
see a whole table filled with gold medals. They were
bigger than his hand and they sparkled in the sunlight.
Toby couldn't wait for them to be given out.

"Gather round," Miss Meadow called,
blowing a big whistle.
"Let's line up in a row to have
our first race. The running race!"

Toby stood beside Charlie, Ellie and Olivia, and they
all got ready to run as fast as they possibly could.

Miss Meadow called out, "Ready, Steady, Go!"
and '*Zoom!*' they ran towards the finish line.

Hooray!

Hooray!

"Whe

eee!"

Charlie yelled as he
crossed the finish line first.

Everybody cheered loudly.
"Well done, Charlie," puffed Toby, a little bit out of breath.
"You were really fast. You'll definitely get a gold medal."

Next it was time for the **egg-and-spoon race**.
It was very tricky!

Wibble! Wobble! Wobble!

"Phew," Toby panted as he got to the end.
"That was close."

Oops!

"This is fun!" giggled Toby as he practised jumping for the sack race.

Bounce!
Bounce!

"Look at how high Poppy can jump," said Olivia. "I'm sure she'll get a medal."

And when they had the race, Poppy jumped **so high** over the finish line that she leapt out of her sack!

Wahoo!

There was a
skipping race...

a relay race...

and a wheelbarrow race.

"I wish it was Sports Day every day," said Toby happily.

Soon it was time for lunch. A table was piled high with towers
of sandwiches, crisps, fruit, buns and yummy-looking biscuits.

Toby had **one** banana...

...**two** carrot sticks,

three cheese sandwiches,

four strawberries

and

five blueberry biscuits.

It was a **LOT** of food.

Everyone had a rest after lunch and Miss Meadow
asked them all to draw a picture. She handed out paper,
pencils and paints, and Toby shared his felt-tip pens.

Toby knew just what to draw – a **gold medal!**
He got straight to work with a yellow felt-tip pen.

After drawing came the best race of all...
the space-hopper race!
Toby and his friends bounced as fast as they
could towards the end of the field.

"Yahoo!" cried Olivia as she bounced over the finish line.

Now everyone had won a race. Everyone, that is, except Toby. He felt a bit funny.
"Well done, Olivia," Toby said, but his voice wobbled.

He blinked hard, trying not to be sad that he wasn't going to get a medal.

Miss Meadow lifted the medals high up in the air.
"Well done! It's time for all of you to get your medals."

"Me, too?" asked Toby in delight.
"But I didn't win anything."

"Everyone gets a gold medal today because you've all worked really hard," smiled Miss Meadow. "And this one's for **you**, Toby!"

Hooray!

Hooray!

Hooray!

So Toby stood proudly in front of Miss Meadow as she hung the shiny gold medal around his neck. The whole class clapped and cheered.

After that, it was time for everyone to go home.
Toby and his friends walked out of the school gates,
their gold medals glinting in the sunlight.

"What a lovely day it's been,"
sighed Toby happily to his mum.
"An extra-special gold medal day!"

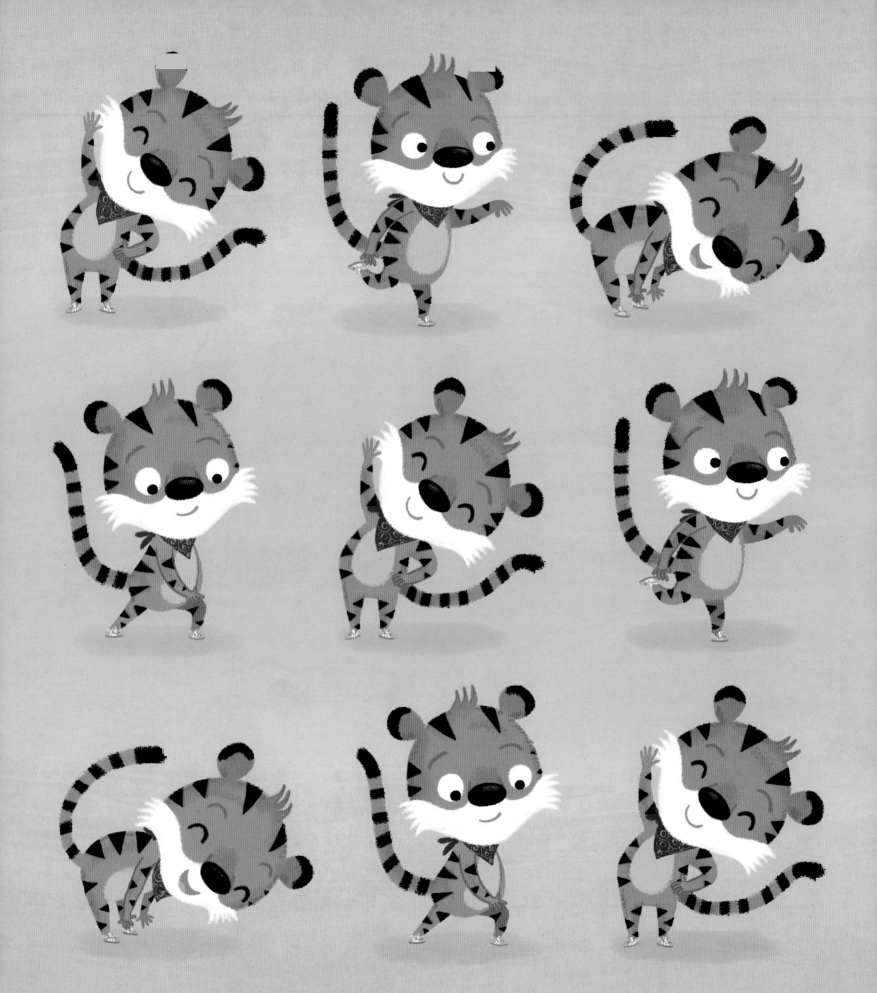

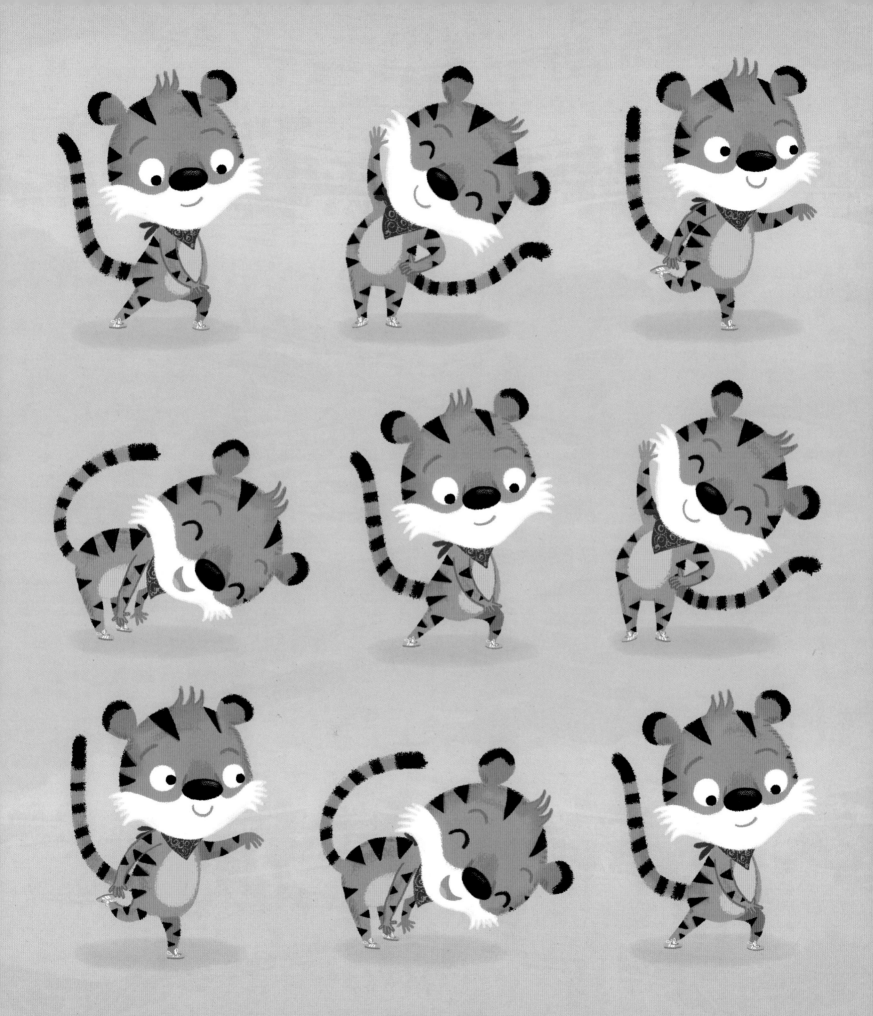